Ava
QUEEN OF
THE FAIRIES

M. L. Ruscsak

Ava, Queen of the Fairies

By: M.L.Ruscsak

AVA QUEEN OF THE FAIRIES

M.L.Ruscsak

COPYRIGHT

Ordering Information:

Quantity sales. Special discounts are available on quantity purchases by corporations, associations, and others. For details, contact the publisher at the address above.

Orders by U.S. trade bookstores and wholesalers. Please contact Trient Press: Tel: (775) 996-3844; or visit www.trientpress.com.

Printed in the United States of America

Publisher's Cataloging-in-Publication data

Ruscsak, M.L.

A title of a book :Ava Queen of the Fairies

For that someone special that

reaches my heart even with the

distance that keeps us apart

AVA QUEEN OF THE FAIRIES

M.L.Ruscsak

Chapter 1

She sat on the tall mountain cliff peering down over the great boulder. Silently she watched and listened. Far below her in the valley, the wild Akhal-Teke were gallantly running, their metallic coats glistening in the pre-dawn light. The sounds of their hooves beating flowing up to her.

Her heat raced in her chest as she watched. Excitement running wild within her thoughts.

It was said that to befriend one was nearly impossible. And to ride one? Oh, only a great fairywarrior would be able to conquer such a feat.

What would those of the village say when she, the smallest fairy, not only rode one of these magicalcreatures but it chose to become her noble beast?

Would they continue to make fun of her? Sneering down their noses? Would they still tell her that her mind was still dancing within the clouds? Willthey still believe that she was best suited for tending the daisies?

No, she wouldn't allow them to continue. Not after she befriended of those great steeds. But she would show them what she had known all of her younglife. She would prove to them that she would be the next great fairy queen.

She was the chosen. She was the Queen who would defend their lands from the invaders. She wouldprotect them from the threat that was still lurking withinthe shadows.

A careful flutter of wings then a light airy huff. "There you are Ava . I knew that I would find you hereinstead of tending to the gardens."

Aleena. The princess of the fairies. The last descendant of the great Queen. Neither title did this fairy deserve. Did her people even know it was Aleenathat was conspiring with the enemy? That she was using her title as princess as a lure to marry one?

Probably not. Or if they did they didn't believe

it.Keeping her eyes fixed on the herd of Akhal-Teke, Ava nodded. "I'm surprised that you haven't tried to befriend one yet."

No one else would have dared to speak as suchto this princess. None except for her.

"Oh tsk. Why would I ever want or need to? I have a glorious pair of wings to take me to whereverthat I wish. Besides, I was born a true princess."

It was meant to be a verbal knife in the gut. Yet, Aleena missed something in her education. A simple truth as damning as anything ever could be. That truth?Being born a princess didn't make you Queen. Actually, no queen had ever been born a princess. This Ava knew. Just as she also knew that the last queen, who lived more then a hundred years ago, had decreed it
on her death bed that none from her line would ever be queen. Her last words had been that a fairy born from those with little power would save their race andbe the greatest queen who had ever been crowned.

"I'll return to the gardens soon. You have myword, Princess Aleena."

Carefully Aleena leaned forward and hissed,"You will never be Queen, little fairy."

AVA QUEEN OF THE FAIRIES

Ava waited until she was sure that she was once again alone. She couldn't wait any longer. Shecouldn't afford to. Her people couldn't afford to live without a great queen or a gallant warrior.

Carefully she fluttered down to the valley, stopping at the edge where the shadows still concealed her movements. There were small foals playing not far from her. It would be easy to approachthem. Easy to gain their trust.

But that wasn't the one that she had been watching. No, she needed a true steed. One that was born a leader. One that knew what it meant to keep hisherd safe. Keeping her hands steady at her side she left the cover of the shadows. The young foals paused in their activities watching her. Ready to bolt as a moment's notice.

The rest of herd would stampede if the little ones were in danger.

She didn't look to any of them. Her eyes fixed on the not the stallion but the mare that every set of equestrian eyes seems to be watching. Her choice was made, now what would the answer be?

Stopping still a few yards away from the mare,Ava bowed her head keeping it lowered as hooves pawed the ground around her. She was an enemy. She was alone. Thoughts battered her. Slowly she rose, her soft voice calm and steady as she said, "I seek no harm from you nor your herd."

There was no telling if the horses could understand her. No movement that told that they understood why she was now standing in the center of a circle created by their shimmering bodies.

Then…

And elderly voice filled her head, "Why are you here, little one?"

It was a female voice. Old and tired.

"My name is Ava . I have come seeking afriend."

"A friend? She seeks to enslave

us.""She's trying to deceive us."

"Run."

Other voices. Other fears. Both young and old. Female and male.

"No. We shall not run. But you are seekingmore then a friend." The old mare said. Ava nodded acknowledging the truth in the mare's words. "It is said among my people only the worthy can befriend the great wild Akhal-Teke. But only the chosen would ride the greatest steed into battle to defend her people."

"And you have come to see the truth in thosewords."

She shook her head. "No, the words are truth. Ithas been the same for many queens. Only they have been able to make friends. Only they rode your kind into battle."

The old silver mare turned, taking but a few steps. "Do you know the bond of my people and yoursis not developed in time of need. Do you know it is thetrust on both parts that lead to the bond that you are seeking?"

"There was much never told about how the queens of old have bonded with their steeds. I wish tolearn more if you will teach me."

"*I* cannot, but my foal, Delmira, she will teachyou. If worthy, she will lead you in to battle."

"I understand. Thank you."

The houses parted just enough for a tall youngmare to be seen. Her color voronaya with marbled eyes; rare for this breed of silver metallic and shimmering golds. Ava held back the gasp of awe.
This was the steed that she had seen in her dreams.

This was the mare that would strike fear into the heartsof the invaders.

Once more she bowed. "Lady Delmira. I ampleased with making you acquaintance."

Delmira pawed the ground once. "She is small. But well mannered. I will teach her and see if she istruly worthy of my friendship."

M.L.Ruscsak

Chapter 2

It felt like weeks had passed since she has started coming here to meet with Delmira. Weeks andshe felt that she had learned nothing that could help.

Invaders nameless and faceless had taken control over several acres of land where the Akhal-Teke roamed free. Several scores of these magnificentcreatures were now either dead or caged. Forced into a kind of slavery that was beyond barbaric.

There was nothing that she alone could do. They needed forces.
Armies.

Her village had those things and there were bound to the will of the queen. And they had no queen so none would form ranks to do anything to lift a finger.

"Ahhh. This is so frustrating. Your Kingsmen need help. Your foals need to escape yet you blame me for their folly." Ava pumped her wings lifting herselffrom the valley floor just a few feet. Just enough to gaze into Delmira's marbled eyes. "You wish to end this come to my village with me. Let me help."

"You are too little, small one. You will have nopower over those who wish harm both your race andmine."

"Why are so blind to see what is standing rightin front of you!" Ava turned and shot into the sky as fast as her wings could carry her. High enough to seeevery last Akhal-Teke that belonged to this herd.

She needed to make a decision. She needed away to show Delmira that she did have the power to protect no only her kind but was worthy of the task of protecting the fairies as well. She needed...

Closing her aqua colored eyes, she let her small body feel with every ounce of power that she could wield. Let herself become one with everything that was around her. The mountains, grass and trees were the life force that she could now feel. The sky anendless void anticipating her every need. And the Akhal-Teke? They were the object that she would protect.

She didn't understand what she had done until she opened her eyes once more. Below her she couldjust make out the edges of a shield as it fell over the valley. Above her something glittered as it caught the sunlight. Carefully she flew beyond her shield. Not a solid as some could make but an illusion. She understood that one she was free from the dome andgazing down.

Far below, Ava knew there were hundreds ofAkhal-Teke grazing. Knew there were foals playing near the small river. Yet, it was only the valley floor that she could see.

Yes, that would do nicely. Or at least for the moment. Later she would have to have do something to keep the enemy out. Later she would have to makethis permanent. But for the moment it would do.

Now to convince Delmira to contact the otherherds and bring them here under the protection of...

There... movement near the trees. Not horses but...

She carefully floated down into the edge of the dome protected from sight yet she could still see everything beyond what she had created. Foul odors came to her, masking the scent of the lilacs and sweet grass.

Theses were the monsters who where huntingher friends. The monsters that Aleena wished to join with. And they were here to hunt those who she had befriended.

Fluttering back to Delmira's side, Ava help her finger to her lips. "Shh. The shield will keep you hiddenbut will not keep out sound. Least not yet."

Carefully Delmira laid in the tall grass. A glanceat the others and they all did the same. Only a few of the foals took a moment long to follow the older of the Akhal-Teke. For a long tense moment none dared to do more than breathe. The intruders stood not more then inches from the edge of the shield. Their short piglike snouts sniffing the air. Yet they did not dwell nor go any further.

They hadn't seen the herd. They didn't find any of the prized stallions or precious foals. Her shield hadsaved them. At least for the moment.

Breathing out a sigh of relief she gave Delmira her most fierce stare. "Will you now come with me to address my people? Or do you prefer to see if they willbe back?"

The old mare took slow measured steps overtoo where they still staring at one another. Both Avaand Delmira waiting for the other to look away first. "Go with her daughter. It is time for our herd to be once again united with the fairies."

Chapter 3

Long ago the last queen of the fairies had hidden the passage that allowed the Akhal-Teke to freely travel between the great village and their ownmeadow. The reason had been simple; She didn't want one befriending any fairy unless it became necessary.

Ava understood this. As she understood many things that others seemed to overlook. Just as she understood that the granddaughter of the once great fairy craved power but lacked the heart to care for herpeople.

Yet today none of that could matter. She had a mission. She had to get Delmira to her village before it became to late to stop the coming war.

Fluttering in front of the great mountain that separated the heard from her village Ava huffed out, "Iknow it is here. I can feel the difference in the stone yet..."

Delmira snorted. "It is a wonder you feel anything at all, little one."

It was true that she was smaller then most fairies but her size didn't hold her back from anything. In fact, it was just the opposite. She small size allowedher to wiggle into spaces no other could fit into. Plus, itallowed her to be unseen by those who only sought out the larger of her kinsman.

A wicked smile bloomed on her face as she faced Delmira. "My size does not hinder my abilities;however…" Glittering light surrounded the both of them. "…Yours does."

A single breath and Delmira stood before Ava pawing at the ground. Her size now only a tenth of what it had been. "What did you do? I demand…"

"Oh hush. The tunnel is not tall enough for a fullsize Akhal-Teke to enter. The spell will wear off once we cross the other side. Now come, I wish to end this quickly."

Leaning her snout closer to Ava , Delmira gritted her teeth. "You are most annoying."

"As are you. Which is why we will work welltogether."

The tunnel had been dark and damp. Creaturesthat had made it their home had scurried away from the light that poured from Ava 's wings. Light that she had never noticed before. Not something that she hadtime to ponder but something that would need to later.

"I smell sweet grass. And a waterfall is

near."This time it was Ava who snorted. "Of

course,
the waterfall is near. Where do you thing the sprite live?"

"Sprite? I know not the name."

Another time Ava might have retorted with some curt remark, but it didn't seem right. Not when Delmira sounded truly confused and wary. "A sprite is a water fairy. Woodland fairies are known as nymphs."

"Then you are …"

"The counsel has not decided what I am. Despite my size I have abilities of all forms of fairy. Yetthey have never truly pondered it either." Ava Stopped at the edge where light was just starting to stream intothe tunnel. "Once you cross fully into the light my spellwill fade and your size will be restored. From here we must go to the Breen; that's the palace. It is partly in the waterfall and partly not."

Taking but a single step forward Delmira bowed her head. "Not many of your kind can speak to my kinsmen. Can they?"

"No. Even among those who can speak to animals only one born every few generations can speak to your race. And from them none have everbeen Queen."

Chapter 4

From the edge of the village Delmira could see the top of the Breen. Golden water cascading down the side. A great tree forming the other. Ivory arches tall enough to accommodate even the tallest of her kind. She could imagine wild flowers climbing the sidesas a welcome feast for her brethren. Her mother had been wise to send her with the tiny fairy. This one didn't crave power. Didn't want more then what she had. No, this one only wanted others to have what they deserved.

The little fairy wanted to protect what the last queen had tried to. She wanted a race not her own tothrive in it's own way. With its own culture and traditions. She wanted them to be free.

Yes, this tiny fairy was the next queen. Shecould see that now.

"You should take your place upon my back, littleone. Let your people see what they have denied for too long."

Ava nearly stumbled over her own feet. Was she really hearing what she thought she had? Had Delmira really suggested that she ride her through thegates of the village and into the Breen? Fluttering to gaze into the marbled eyes of Delmira she saw the truth. All of the bantering. All of the annoying remarks.All of the doubt. Delmira had been pushing her to this moment. Preparing her to face away any doubts that her people, not the Akhal-Teke might have. "Would you mind if I create a seat?"

"Saddle, little one. Not a seat. There is still much I teach you."

Yes, there was. She couldn't deny that, but withthem working together maybe those things would be easier explained. Nodding once she fluttered to Delmira's side and closed her eyes.

She had heard stories about the saddles used by the former queens. Strong and sturdy. Elegant yet bold. Battle ready yet something they could use just tofrolic with their friends.

She had never seen a saddle and till now didn'tknow the proper word. Yet in her mind she could see itto perfectly. Fine leather made not from hides but frompressed Raffia Palm. Buttons of ivory holding the layers together at the seams. The seat padded with sage and mulleins. The skirt made from woven chenille.

Slowly she opened her eyes and gazed at amasterpiece. "Does it feel ok? Not to tight?"

"I can barely notice anything at all. Only a softwarmth. You did well Little Queen."

Tears stung her eyes. After years of seeing what was wrong within not only her village but beyondthe great mountain she may finally have a way to change it.

Her kinsmen whispered as she passed. Her eyes locked straight ahead. Let them whisper. Let them deny what they see with their own two eyes. Letthem…

An old fairy guard stepped out in front of her. She had known him her entire life. Tyro, the of the queen's guards. Keeper of the great army of fairies. And only living fairy to have said to actually have seenthe queens saddle. "Tyro, I…"

"So, my little warrior has finally found her saddleand such a beautiful mare to wear it."

Ava shook her head in disbelief. "Tyro?"

"Did you really think I did not notice you watching as the army trained? Or when you started barking orders to change a great many things that onlya true queen would see or care about? No, my little one I see now that perhaps you were the only one not ready to see the truth of what you are."

"You knew. For these past few years you knewyet you allowed for Aleena to have her way!?" Ava gasped. "Why?"

"She is a princess and only a queen can standin her way." Slowly he turned to head up the white stone path to the Breen. "Come now child, let this oldman show the rest of our people what I have long seen."

Chapter 5

Carefully Ava rode into the Breen. She glanced quickly at the elaborate tapestries of battles fought by previous queens. Saw the golden armor forged by the magic of those same queens. Elvin blades hung in cases. Their steel still as sharp today as it was the daythat it had been created. The magic held within the steel… legendary.

But today was not the day to stare in awe at thebeauty of the Breen. No, today was the day that the counsel would either except her as the true queen andthey would yield to her will. They would muster the army and face the enemy forces.

Or they would cast her out, choosing to ignore the threat until it much too late to do anything about it.

No. No, she would never allow them to cast herout. Not even if it meant going against the wishes of the counsel and doing what needed to be done.

"Master Tyro, what does the commander of thegreat army bring into the Breen?"

She couldn't see the face that belonged that deep cultured voice but she understood this must be the grand master of the counsel. His voice, his wishes out ranked the others. It would be his vote that she would need to win in order to do what was needed.

Tyro stepped into the large circle that was far below where the counsel sat lazily upon their flowered seats. "I have bore witness to the rise of the last queenof our proud people. And I have witness the decline since her passing."

Hushed murmurs filled the room. Echoes bouncing off of the stone walls drowning out the cascading water that fell outside.

"For years I have waited until the next queenwould rise."

Hands slapped the balcony far above where Tyro stood. Thunder filling the room. "There will be noqueen."

Anger raged thru her. Cold and burning. She knew that voice. It was the father of Princess Aleena.He was the grandmaster. He was…

Urging Delmira forward, Ava growled, "What right do you have to declare that there will be no queen? What right do you have to deny what your owndaughter has done to buy you a seat at this counsel? Ihave heard the tales of your own mother. I have heardthe orders that she herself gave so that you would bare no power over her people."

"Silence!!!"

Letting go of the few strands of golden mane, Ava fluttered up to the balcony where the twelve fairiesof the counsel watched her. Twelve sets of eyes but only one seemed furious. "You cannot silence me. I won't allow it, Adan. I will not allow for your child to enslave those of the Akhal-Teke. And I will not allow you to remain as grandmaster of a counsel when you were to be banished for the death of your mother."

Ava stopped stunned that she had said thosewords out loud. How could have known all that she had said? How…

Light poured into her. Dripped from her in specks of dust covering the floor below. This was thedoing of a queen. Not a born queen but of a chosen one. One that the stars had placed upon this earth toguide her people. There was no denying her words now.

There was no denying that she was the Queen.

This was a gift not even the last great queen had had. She the gift of stars and only honest wordscould ever pass her lips. Her knowledge from this moment would never be questioned. Couldn't be.

Fire sizzled past her. Warm air surrounded her.

AVA QUEEN OF THE FAIRIES

Adan. How had she forgotten that he was a fairy of fire? How could she had forgotten that she would try to destroy her to save himself and his little princess?

Her vision hazed for just a moment. He wasn'ttrying to save himself, he was however trying to destroy her in a massive ball of fire. Yet… the flamesdidn't touch her skin. The heat nothing more then a warm summer's breeze. He was trying, that she understood. But, she was the queen. One of great power and she had yet to test any of those powers.

Until now.

A deep breath and she called the flames to her,snuffing them out completely. Her eyes now dancing with embers. Her voice deeper then it once been. "Guards, seize the former grandmaster of the counsel."

She never knew where they had come from. Never saw them enter but there just before her were hundreds of fairy warriors all battle ready. Two haulingAdan from the council chambers and presumably into the dungeon to await further instructions.

The younger fairy that had been seated to Adan's left slowly rose from her seat. Her head inclined to acknowledge the queen who stood beforeher. "Never in the history of our people had a traitor ever sat on the counsel. It saddens my heart to knowthat the son of our great queen was the first." She lifted her head now to gaze into Ava 's eyes. "How canthe fairy counsel assist you my queen?"

She needed assistance for several things. Firstto being too quiet her racing heart that she was sure every fairy in this room could hear. But that needed towait. Least for a moment maybe two.

Her eyes gazed at the room as she slowly turned in a circle. Fairy blades already sharpened. Warriors already prepared to defend. So many lives held with in this room. Some may not return home after this battle. Others? Would they be proud that theyserved her or think her as a fool? It was too soon to tellbut there was only one way to find out.

In clear voice she began to speak. "Our friendsthe Akhal-Teke are being attacked. I know not what the creatures that hunt them are called only what theylook like. There is a temporary shield hiding a small herd of them just outside the queen's tunnel."

"Are we to defend the herd?"

"No. We are to find the creatures that are hunting them. Aleena is at their command. She mustbe stopped."

No one questioned her. Yet they did not move either. For a princess to harm another race it was unheard of. For one with the powers that she possessed to cause their bloodshed, it was an unholyact.

Slowly a guard approached her. "You want the princess…" He didn't finish the question since he wasn't sure what should be done about her.

"For now, I want her alive in the dungeon. Butfirst we need to get the rest of the herds some wheresafe. More of their blood should not be shed for her gain."

Ava watched at the fairy guard scrambled from the Breen. Watched at the counsel left to send messages that a new queen has risen. Still it left her indisbelief. All of this couldn't really be this easy. And even it was… what was she going to do now?

There were till the pig face things hunting the Akhal-Teke. There were still things that needed to befixed within her own village. There was…

Growing to herself she fluttered down sitting on the glitter covered floor just before Delmira. "What am Igoing to do?"

"What did you think would happen, LittleQueen?"

"I -I don't know? I just needed for the counsel to do something. Once my people were revered for things that they could do. The armies were fearsome and just the mention of them would strike fear in thosewho would do harm to our allies. But I don't actually know how to go from this moment to where I think things should be." Ava paused, "I guess I always thought the queen would just know the answer and everyone would just follow her. I never really thought about how she actually came up with the answers."

Touching her muzzle to Ava 's head, Delmira snorted hot air into her face. "You are little and have not yet lived long enough to know the answers. But that doesn't mean you don't understand the questions." She paused, "You will have many failures.But you will also have many successes. This comes with time and with wisdom from learning from what work for you."

Flinging her arms around Delmira's neck Avasniffled, "How is it that you are so wise?"

AVA QUEEN OF THE FAIRIES

"My mother is the alpha mare. But do not tell my father I told you. He still thinks that it is he that runs the herd."

Wiping her face, she let out a little giggle. "Oh, I would never say a word." Looking around the empty room she listened to the waterfall rushing down the side of the Breen. Felt the leaves of the great tree swaying in the wind. Her senses heightened. Something was coming… Something…

…

The ground rumbled and stone shook loose from the ceiling.

"Delmira!!!" Melisa shouted

"We must run." Rocks crumbled as they hit the ground. Too quickly she raised up onto her hind legs and squealed. "Now!!!"

Too quickly she was gripping Delmira's saddle and racing from the Breen. Every moment she hoped that it would fall in on top of her. Every breath filled
with both fear and rage as her thoughts battered at her.

Golden light filled the main door just as the roaring wind ceased. A few pebbled more fell from being shaken loose from the great tree. Then a horrible silence filled the air.

There was nothing that made Ava want to take the lastfew steps into that light. Night would ever make her want to… yet…

… she was queen. Not just a queen but THEQUEEN. She had to show confidence and face the threat no matter what it may be.

Patting Delmira's neck she leaned close to herear. "Careful. I do not know what is out there but the air feels strange."

A bobbled nod and the great Akhal-Teke pulled herself to her full height nearly taking the whole of thecovered entrance. Her body filling most of the door asshe slowly stepped into the light.

M.L.Ruscsak

Chapter 6

The light was blinding so much more then that from the sun. In shock she covered her eyes with her thin arm hoping to be able to see the cause. Hoping tofind the source and…

Ava gasped as her vision cleared. The grand waterfall had split open revealing the lost river of the elves. In it's place a massive ship Shimmering silver and golden sails. Glittering green emblems marking itas the royal ship of the elven kingdom.

She had never seen such a magnificent sight. Never had she heard tails of the grand ships. Yet sheknew just by gazing upon it who and what must be onboard.

"My friend can you take me to where they would depart?"

No words slipped from Delmira. Not a single sound of caution or warning. Just her hooves carefullystepping on the freshly crushed stones. Just the sounds around her of the Fairy army hurrying to reachthe ship before their queen.

Her skin pricked with worry. True it was elvenweapons that her people used in time of battle. True none had better armor then those made from the greatroyal elves themselves. But this didn't feel like a ship coming to sell it's wears. It didn't feel like …

She didn't have time to figure out what it felt likefor the elven bugles rang out greeting not her but their royal family. Forest green robes clocked them. Three. Yes, she could see three standing at the side of the ship. An opening for a ramp, yet none appeared.

Slowly with nothing more then a breezy wave ofher fingers the ground moved up to the opening. A blanket of red clover covering the dirt as it greeted the edge of the ship. Not knowing what to say, Ava cantered over to the end of the aisleway and let the wind carry her voice. Hoping all the while not to offendthis royal family.

"Greetings, friends. And welcome to the village of my people."

The taller of the three held his hand so that the elf next to him may depart first. Accepting his offer narrow fingers unfastened the cape allowing it to fall tothe ground. Blowing long brown hair and the sliver circlet of the elven kingdom adorn upon her head.
Carefully she made her way down the ramp stoppingonly once she stood nearly eye to eye with Delmira.

"You're majesty?" Ava gave a bobbled bow from her seat not yet wishing to move from her perch.

"You are much smaller than the last queen of this village, but we have means to fix that. But that canwait."

Her voice was noting more then a summer's breeze. Light and airy. Warm like the first true day of spring. It sounded friendly yet… there was something within the eyes that warned Ava not to trust blindly. Anelven queen wouldn't have left her kingdom without cause. "We are honored at your arrival. However, I ampuzzled at the timing."

The elven queen smiled then let out a small laugh, "Are you always so callus in your words, littlequeen? You give away much with them."

Give away what? She had asked more or lessto the reason that elven kingdom was docked within the water way.

"Even so…" the queen continued, "Maybe weshould begin with the introductions. Yes?"

A deep breath and Ava swallowed the words that burned within her throat. She was queen not just afairy. She needed to master when to speak formal andwhen to speak truthfully. "I am Ava . Queen of this village and all of the Fairy army."

"And I am, Osonia Kelxidor. Queen and high elfof the Elven kingdom." She turned acknowledging the tall lean man who was ever so slowly approaching. "My husband and grand weapons maker, Keryth." Turning her to Ava she smiled, "You have been queenfor mere moments. Where I have been queen for a thousand years. You little one, do not know the nuances of our kingdom so it is up to me to teach you.Now come we shall speak within the Breen and my husband can tinker with bits of metal for you army."

"You have done this before then. Aided thequeen of the fairies?"

"Little one, the last queen and I were grand friends. My kingdom withdrew from yours on day of herdeath. There was much wrongness with day. Enough that had not wished to aid you now."

"Her son and only child killed her. I think he washoping that his daughter would become queen even if his mother had foretold otherwise." Then the rest of what Osonia said sank in. "You knew that and you sealed off the gateway to the valley of the Akhal-Teke as well as that of your own kingdom."

"I did. And if not for my own son I would have allowed for them both to remain hidden no matter theprice."

Tea and nectar was served in the Breen nearthe waterfall. Cups made of tulips and plates made from woven sweet grass. I wasn't fantasy. Wasn't something that she had ever thought about … but now…

Glancing over her tulip cup Ava tried to smile,"Is tea to your liking, Osonia?"

"You are but a strange one. No matter. You have no royal to guide you. No hand to be there to teach all that you need. Perhaps it is good that my sonhas a such fondness for horses and has urged me to help."

This was the second time the great elven queenhad mentioned her son. And the second time that she sounded contrite at being told what to do. "You son sounds wise to wish give aid to those who are helpless."

"Either wise beyond his years or not. We shall see once this mater is dealt with." Osonia paused pressing her lips into the thin lines. "Do you know whoit is that threatens both your people and the darling horses?"

Ava nodded once. "Princess Aleena. She led the attackers to where the Akhal-Teke were hidden."

"Yes, dear that is a very distressing matter. However, is that really the threat that I am speaking. Surly needing to save some silly horse was not the reason for the fairies to once again feel the need for aqueen."

Ava narrowed her eyes trying to decide what this great queen was really saying. The answer came to her with equivalent of a fist to her chest. Gasping she pushed away from the table. Several dishes beingknocked to the floor from the current of her translucentwings.

Her seat tumbled to the cold ground as she floated just a breath away from the floor. "You. It was you that gave Aleena the power to create those monsters."

Easing from her seat Osonia gave Ava a rueful smile, "Very good little queen. But why…"

"What did you do?"

A dark tenor voice came from behind her. The voice she didn't know but it was clear from the flash offear that Osonia did. And the great queen hadn't beenexpecting whoever it was to walk in during this conversation.

Soft foot falls on smooth garnet floor. The sound of the chair that had been turned on his side being up righted. A sideways glance and her heart raced but not with fear but in awe. Here beside her was the prince of the elven kingdom. A man about herown age and breathtakingly handsome. Later she would need to speak to him right now she needed to be the queen that her people needed.

"Your mother was just explaining why she helped Aleena create the monsters that are nowhunting the Akhal-Teke."

Elyon crossed his narrow arms, "First off for proper introductions. Osonia is queen and did help to seal off the port between our two kingdoms. However, she is not my mother nor is she even a high elf. You having tea with her is merely so that I can have a goodlook at what has became of a once flourishing kingdom." He took a deep breath and his scowl deepened, "And she will be dealt with for the pain that she has caused on innocent creatures."

Ava watched as he gave a small flick of hiswrist calling forth a trove of armed guards. Their magical spears all pointed at their queen.

Swallowing hard she tried to smile, "Prince Elyon perhaps we should walk while your people deal withher?"

There was nothing friendly in his eyes. Nothinghuman. And certainly not anything that she wanted to be looking at her for very long. Then he blinked once and sly smile formed on his metallic rose lips. "I think that would be a welcome idea. Since we still need to deal with the current threat to your kingdom."

Chapter 7

It seemed like forever that they slowly walked around the whole of the village. Even longer to reach agreat willow tree that still stood guarding the entrance of the once golden gates of the village. Carefully Elyonreached up and caressed a long leafy vine. So lovely. So tender.

"I would apologize for Osonia. But in reality, there is no excuses for the likes of her."

She could dismiss it or she could ask all of thequestions that burned in her throat. "She's not your mother but…"

Elyon snorted, "My mother is the high elf of the elven counsel. Make no mistake there is no other morepowerful then she. My father was chosen to be my sirethough I can not phantom why. Yet he was given the title of king."

"So, for the sake of appearance your kingdomhas a King that travels making great weapons. But only those close to the elven …um… family… wouldknow that it is a title in name only."

"In truth yes. We rarely tell outsiders how out kingdom is run. And only those who are trusted knowwhat I have just told you."

Why? She couldn't ask that. Nodding once shesmiled, "Then I am greatly honored that you told me."

Sliding his fingers thru his long dark hair, Elyon hesitated before answering, "Yes well, my mother sentme here after I'm assuming figuring out what Osonia had been up to. And since the named queen is responsible for this mess I'm choosing the simplest way to fix at least some of it."

He may look like a man but he was still a boy. Or at least acted like one when around her. It was a comfort knowing that he had a delicate side after seeing what she recognized as a threat before. "That Iappreciate. However, what do you suggest for handling Aleena and her creations?"

"Since we have no idea how many creations that she has now at her feet. I'm afraid the only way to end this is to defeat her. An Elven sword to the heart should in theory end all of those that she created usingour magic." Elyon paused biting the corner of his pale lips. "Or at least in theory. As this has never happenedbefore, we don't have a real way of knowing until after."

What? He couldn't have just said that. He couldn't have just told her that she had to kill another fairy with the tone of speaking of the weather. Yet...

Her stomach burned with the truth.

Elyon was telling her the truth in the simplest way that he could. Or perhaps he just didn't have theexperience of saying the truth without blurting out thefirst words that came to his mind. Both were a very true possibility.

Yet it didn't make announcing this to herkingdom any easier.

Calming herself, Ava stepped out on the grandbalcony of the Breen. Far below her the great fairy army stood proudly waiting for their order. Delmira was off to the side laying in the tall grass allowing small children to place newly formed flowers in her mane. All of this she saw. Yet she saw nothing at all.

AVA QUEEN OF THE FAIRIES

She couldn't look at any of them while she spoke. She wouldn't allow herself to see their disappointment once she was done. Her heart achedfor all of the self-doubts that she now had. Taking a slow deep breath, she let her translucent wing lift herfor the balcony. A single breath more and she let thewords flow from her lips.

"Citizens of our great fairy village. For far too long we have diluted ourselves in trusting one that isthe descendant of our great queen. I am horrified to learn that it was she who created the monsters that now attack the Akhal-Teke."

Stunned gasped flowed up to her. Hushed murmurs. Wishers hoping that what she was sayingwasn't true. Couldn't be true. Despair. So many disheartened. Grief for the once queen who's own offspring could have turned so horribly wrong.

Trying to quit the fears and the sorrow Ava softly gestured for the crown to quite once more. Her wings not fluttering with distress but with a calm that she had to maintain. "We will find Aleena and end thiswar that she is creating."

"How do we know it is Aleena who is behind thedeaths of the Akhal-Teke? How do know that is was not all a ploy for *Ava* to become queen?"

She wasn't sure who said it. Then again it really didn't matter since this was one of her fears.

"Would you dare question the word of your queen? Words that once the power of your Breen hasfilled her can not be used to lie?" That dark voice … she knew that voice. Still it took her a moment longer to recognize the Elven warrior who was slowly approaching her side. Probably wouldn't have recognized him at all if he had kept his metal leaf helmet on.

Elyon. The heir to the Elven kingdom. The boy who had shy spots when they were alone. The battle-ready man who stood before her now ready to plunge his sword into any how dared to side with Aleena. Yes,she could see that in his scowl.

Only one way to defuse the tension between the two kingdoms. "Prince Elyon is correct. My words can not be manipulated. Nor can I lie. Not that I ever have before. We all know the legend of the last Fairy queen. We all know it was her one son who took her life. This same son ceased control of the counsel. Thevery man who fathered Aleena and poisoned her mindso that she wanted … lusted for… until she found someone who was willing to give her the gift to create those horrid monsters. It is up to us to end this."

M.L.Ruscsak

Chapter 8

The Akhal-Teke were hidden away. Many on shipsbound for the arc of the high council of the Elven kingdom.Others protected with in the Breen itself. Strong strange magic protected them now. Even if she failed those beautiful creatures that she had long ago fell in love with would be spared. They would go on forever protected by the high counsel of elven kingdom. Some would go to far way land and would only be known as the most exotic of equestrian flesh that any had ever seen.

Regardless of when took place today. One promise would be kept. The Akhal-Teke would onceagain be safe.

Ava readied herself for battle. An elven spear in her right hand the reins of Delmira's bridle in her left. The fairy army and those who came from the elven kingdom were nothing more than a sea of silver just barely behind her. Hoof beats and the sea of bodies parted just to her left. A heartbeat more and Elyon saton the finest charger that she had ever seen.

"I'm surprised that none of the Akhal-Teke wouldnot choose for you to ride them on this day."

Elyon narrowed his eyes as he glared at her. "Iam not a fairy. Nor do I wish to be a fairy."

It was a serious day. A very serious moment that would define so many lives after the battel was over. Still she could not keep her lips from curving intoa ghost of a smile. "We shall see after today."

Ava stared out across the valley. Rows upon rows of creatures. Some appearing with the face of anorc and the body of fabled monsters. Others… Pig snouts and bodies of apes. Each terrifying in its own way. Their weapons… spiked clubs and fails. A few held spears.

But she has seen some of those here up close. She knew without a doubt what they lacked in brain they made up for in brawn. And with Aleena controllingthem anything was possible.

A slow shift of the monsters' bodies. A pure white stallion. Not a glorious Akhal-Teke. Not a breed that she knew. But for whatever it was … it was bewitched with the same curse at the monsters. She could tell by the glowing red eyes of the poor creature.She could feel it no more wanted to be there then a tree wanted to be uprooted by the wind.

Somehow, she would need to make this right…somehow…

"You couldn't leave well enough alone could you… Ava ? Couldn't let the blasted Akhal-Teke perishso there would be no other to be crowned queen otherthan me."

Aleena's voice was carried on the wind to her. Venomlaced within her words.

M.L.Ruscsak

Chapter 9

Sounds of battle cling to her ears. Swords clanged. Metal clashing with metal. Horrid screams coming from the creatures. Elves barking orders. Thefairy warriors keeping to the skies with their freshly made bows. Too many bodies to follow. Too many small battles being fought on this vast field that not long ago held tall sweet grass and wildflowers.

But none of that mattered right now. Couldn'tmatter.

Somewhere out there was Aleena. Somewhereshe would be watching and waiting until she could safely charge into battle and wield whatever elven magic that had been given to her.

Her eyes scanned the field. Slowly they lingeredon the tree line.

There. There hidden within the shadows was the dethroned princess. The monster who had wanted

AVA QUEEN OF THE FAIRIES

to rule without ever understanding why she was notmeant to.

It was a short distance by flight. But it would leave her open for an attack. Rubbing Delmira's neck,Ava leaned forward and yelled over the noise, "There.The tree line."

Delmira didn't waste words nor time just took offin a dead bolt across the raging battle. She didn't stop for those who tried to attack. Didn't dare slow down as she weaved in and out of the sea of creatures. Her only mission was to get to the tree line… to get Ava to the foul creature that created this wasted war.

The ground came up to her much too fast. Hershoulder hit the ground as she slid on the trampled grass. Dazed Ava tied to remember what had happened. One moment she had been racing acrossthe field riding on Delmira's back and the next….

… Pain zinged through her as her saw the blood dripping from her shoulder. A single bolt fromAleena's bow now stuck into her skin. Her vision swayed for just a moment. Her head reeling from disbelief.

A slow movement beside her just out of reach. Delmira. Still alive but badly injured. Her voronaya peltshowing from under the regal elven armor. Her marbled eyes flickering open in shock.

Relief washed through her. Delmira would be ok. She would be…

"Ready to end this little fairy?"

Shit. How in that moment of shock and disbeliefhad she forgotten about the threat? How had she forgotten about Aleena and the stolen magic that she now possessed?

Slowly her hands balled int fist as Ava slowly tried to get to her feet. Her strength gone, yet she hadto try. She had to push forward and defeat this merciless creature. "You will not get away with this."

Slowly Aleena stood before her. No elven armorprotecting her. Just one of their blades. The blade that had belonged to the last queen of the fairies. "My darling I already have."

AVA QUEEN OF THE FAIRIES

The tip of the sword moved, posed to strike Avaonce it came down. This would be how she died. Defeated by her own drive to protect those who wouldnot … could not… protect themselves.

She flinched only once then a terrible sound. Asword connecting with bone. A thud before her as metal clashed clanging onto a nearby rock. Sounds ofbattle fading. A warn sword hilt being pressed into hercold hands.

Just before her world went dark She caught theglimpse of Elyon. A cruel smile twitching on his lips.

Chapter 10

She had opened her eyes in a well-furnished room. Soft curtains blowing in the breeze. A warm blanket covering her. Her armor polished and setting on a tulip chair near the door. Outside she could hearthe waterfall gently cascading into the lagoon.

Slowly she sat up touching where Aleena's bolthad pierced skin. Only not nothing more then a dull ach remained.

"It is about time that you should wake."

The voice sounded tired but blunt all the same. As hereyes adjusted to the light of the hallway Ava took a deep breath, "Prince Elyon?"

Pushing off the frame of the door he took a measured step into the room. "I thought perhaps you would like to know what was told to your people beforeI return to my home."

Something wasn't right here but then again …
"Yesplease."

"I kept it simple since lies are not common among my people. So, for the sake of yours I simply said Aleena struck you with a poisoned bolt and something knocked Delmira off her feet. Then beforethe poison rendered completely helpless you somehow managed to end her with the royal elven sword that I made for you before battle."

"You told…" Ava paused considering her next words carefully, "why did you not take the credit for what you had done?"

Elyon shrugged, "I do not want to be known as the savior of the horses and the keeper of the Breen. Thatis your dream Ava . Not mine."

Elyon had left days ago. As had the elven armthat had come to help defend the Akhal-Teke. Her people were once again safe. The majestic horses were once again free to roam their homelands and frolic within valley not far from the Breen. But today she couldn't think of any of that.

No today she had to be the queen and listen once again to the bickering of the counsel. Today shehad to…

Her hands slammed down on the smooth wood banister that was before her. The sound a crackling thunder throughout the room silencing everyone almost instantly. "No! You will not end lives that did notask to be created."

"My queen…Surely…"

She didn't know his name. Least not yet but thelook on her face was enough for him to swallow anything that he had been about to argue.

Closing her eyes, she stood then let her wings carry her into the center of the great room. Into the center of the counsel. "I do not argue that the creatures should never have given life. However, just because something is not wanted does not give us theright to destroy it."

"The queen is correct."

It wasn't a voice of any of the council members.The stunned gasps confirmed that. Slowly she turned seeing Elyon standing at the back near the royal entrance way lurking within the shadows. But it was the tall thin elf with long golden hair that held her eyes.

AVA QUEEN OF THE FAIRIES

Osonia had been pretty. But this woman. Thiscreature had was so exotic that words such as stunning and beautiful did not due her justice. The golden circlet sitting delicately upon her crown… Slowly Ava swallowed.

Carefully she let her wings carry her back to the balcony and to her seat. "Your grace?" She gave a bobbled curtsy not sure what else to do at the moment.

"Come child. My son shall settle the matter of the poor creatures. We queens have much to discuss."

It wasn't until they were over looking the valleyof the Akhal-Teke That the elven queen spoke once again. "I would like to tell you something that none outside the high counsel of my kingdom knows."

Confused Ava made to delicate seats of thefinest blue bells that she could remember. "Thank you."

Taking a seat, the queen began to softly speak."The last queen and I knew each other well. I had watched her from the time when she had just learned to flutter with the butterflies and dance with the song birds. She came to my kingdom shortly after to learn tobe the queen that your people needed."

Ava raised her hand slightly, "I thought she became queen because she befriended the Akhal-Teke?"

"She did. But for that, she sought out knowledge. She didn't; want to see the darling horsesuntil she knew that she would be worthy to call one friend."

"So… she had training to be a well-versed queen." Disappointment laced Ava 's words. Just the same as the knowledge that Elyon had won her the battle.

"In part. Mostly I taught her the confidence thatshe lacked. And where to trust those who wish to seeher succeed. I told her the same that I will tell you now… a man in love will lurk the shadows if it keeps his beloved safe. "

Her head snapped up, "Elyon?"

"Figured it out that quickly. So, my son must notkeep his intentions as well hidden as he thinks." Laughter filled her voice before she looked away, "but before we speak of him. There is another truth that youmust know."

Nodding once Ava leaned in her heart pounding.

It didn't matter what else this queen said she wantedto get back to the part about Elyon.

"Not long after the last queen …um… well became queen… a child was brought before us. I knew almost instantly that she was born of both theblood of elf and a fairy."

What does…that…

"With your queen's blessings I named her in tradition of my people. I named her Ava ."

She was the only one named …Ava … "Me. You named me?"

"I did. But the name holds a different meaningwithin my kingdom."

From the time that she met this queen she hadn't felt nervous. Hadn't felt like the world would crumbled at her feet. But now. "And what does it meanin your kingdom?"

"Only the High Elf can be named Ava . And onlythe current high elf can give a child that coveted name."

"So, you name is…"

"Eva."

Epilogue

The golden rays of the autumn dawn crept across her face. Warming her despite the bite in thecrisp air. Sounds drifted up from out her window.
Children playing. The Akhal-Teke cheerfully whinnying.

So much had changed since early spring. No longer was she the tiny fairy with abilities unknown. No,she was the Queen of the fairies. Beloved by most but trusted by all. Her words never faltered nor could they be manipulated. Her instincts as a queen growing every day.

The fact that she had elven blood seeping within her veins… ah well no one was perfect but it wasn'tthat bad either.

A soft caught from the door way and she let hereyes lazily flutter open to the man who had captured her heart. The prince of the Elven kingdom. "Elyon?"

"I was beginning to think you would sleep until Icarried you to the ship."

He wouldn't. Looking deep into his eyes… "Youwould, wouldn't you?"

"Mmm. If my darling wishes to sleep until wearrive at our kingdom who am I to argue?"
AVA QUEEN OF THE FAIRIES

He meant that as a compliment. She knew it buthe was still testing the preverbal waters of courtship.

Trying to figure out what to say and when. That she understood. Just as she understood that he was well versed in fighting and making things with his hands. Neither skill required much talking.

Slipping out of her bed she let her finger caressher cheek. "Your kingdom Elyon. We are going to seeyour homeland now that mine is safe. And one day it will be our home."

Too quickly he pulled her close to him needing to hold her. Needing a moment that was just theirs. "Ifthat is what you want."

"Today all I want is the man who would stay inthe shadows to give my people the queen that they needed."

A slow sly smile formed on his lips. "Then I guess it is good that elven men are excellent at lurkingin the shadows and protecting those that they love."

A quick kiss and she pulled his hand. "We better go find Delmira. I doubt she will wish to miss seeing the kingdom that came to her kin's aid."